*for Jasmijn*
*and Imme*

This is an Em Querido book
Published by Levine Querido

www.levinequerido.com · info@levinequerido.com
Levine Querido is distributed by Chronicle Books, LLC

Library of Congress Cataloging-in-Publication data is available.
ISBN 978-1-64614-128-9
Printed and bound in China

MIX
Paper from
responsible sources
FSC
www.fsc.org
FSC™ C104723

Published in March 2022
First Printing
Book design by Christine Kettner
The text type was set in ITC Espirit Std Medium

The drawings in *You Are the Loveliest* are like a color palette, comparable to the moods of a small child that can quickly switch from light to dark. As a cook in a kitchen, Marit Törnqvist came up with a new recipe for each poem, using materials from gouache and acrylic paint to charcoal and ink, from watercolor to pastels, in an attempt to build a child's world from the ingredients that the child immediately has around them. The tower of the church, the sidewalk on the street, the stairs and the wooden floor. The hugs and the books. The neighbor's dog.

This publication has been made possible with financial support from
the Dutch Foundation for Literature.

N ederlands
letterenfonds
dutch foundation
for literature

# You are the Loveliest

# You are the Loveliest

## HANS & MONIQUE HAGEN

ILLUSTRATED BY **MARIT TÖRNQVIST**

TRANSLATED BY **DAVID COLMER**

**LQ**
LEVINE QUERIDO

MONTCLAIR · AMSTERDAM · HOBOKEN

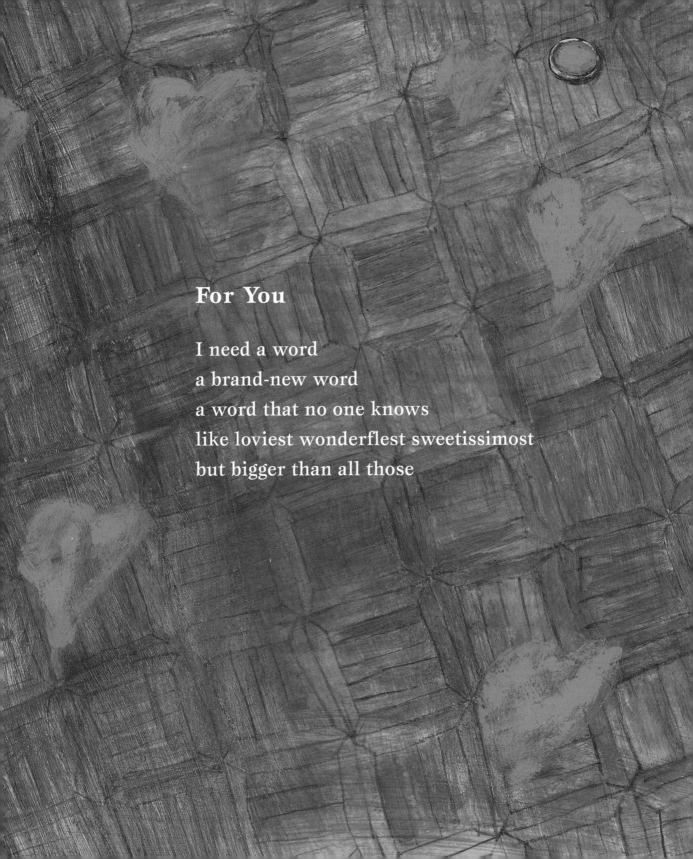

## For You

I need a word
a brand-new word
a word that no one knows
like loviest wonderflest sweetissimost
but bigger than all those

## Dreams

when the day has slipped away
my head sinks on the pillow
and I dream
that I can do as I please
and be every kind of *me* there is
until tomorrow
but there's one thing I won't need
a little cup to cry in
a little cup of sorrow

## 1-2-3

yes is sí
and no is no
and para contar you go
uno-dos-tres
one-two-three

tú is you
and mí is me
mucho is lots
and nada is none

see?
¡sí!
words are fun

# Invisible

sighs are invisible
just like the wind
night is invisible
when daytime begins
the things that I've lost
and really can't find
are invisible
but what I make up
is all visible
when I close my eyes

## Big Feet

my new shoes
are so big
they'll carry this girl
all over the world

# Freesia

baby baby sound asleep
baby baby not a peep
pinch your nose
and don't breathe deep
I think we need a flower

in a vase beside your bed
change it every hour
even if your diaper's full
you'll smell like a flower

### Doggy

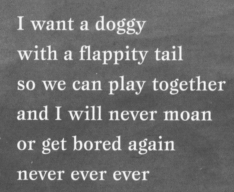

I want a doggy
with a flappity tail
so we can play together
and I will never moan
or get bored again
never ever ever

I want a doggy
with a happity tail
one for keeps not to borrow
and I will always always
always look after him
yesterday, today and tomorrow

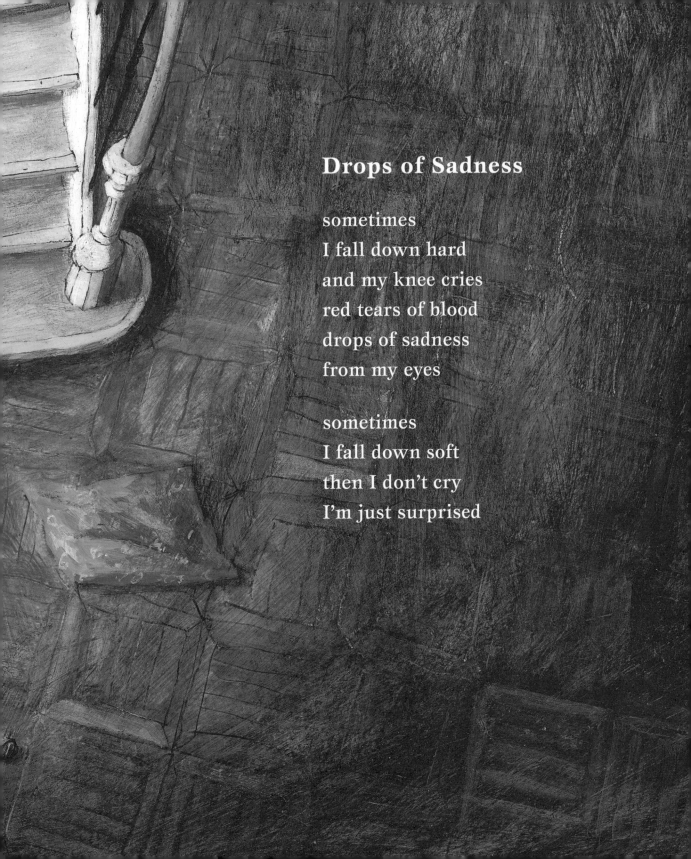

## Drops of Sadness

sometimes
I fall down hard
and my knee cries
red tears of blood
drops of sadness
from my eyes

sometimes
I fall down soft
then I don't cry
I'm just surprised

## Little

a baby dog is called a puppy
a little cow's a calf
a baby bed is called a crib
a quarter's not a half

a baby plant is called a cutting
a tiny fly's a gnat
a little man is still a man
nothing changes that

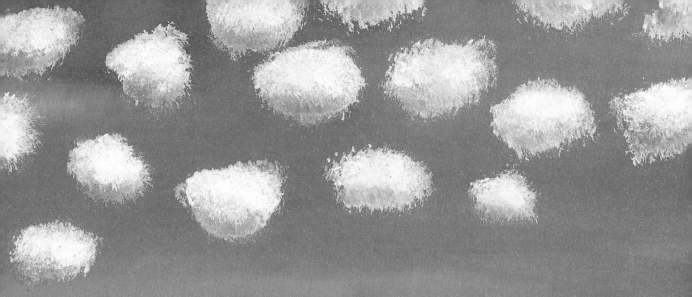

## Clouds

how do clouds stay up
are they made of cotton
or are they made of fluff
can you catch them
with a rod or a hook

why are clouds so high
why do they float by
how come there's never
a curious cloud
that stops for a closer look

## Come On Sun

come on sun
turn your sunbeams on
paint the gray sky blue

hit the clouds with your rays
and chase them all away

a little sunlight on my skin
will be sure to make me grin

come on sun
turn your spotlight on
then I can play tag with my shadow

# Sunflower Sea

sunflowers turn
to follow the sun
they all turn their heads
to follow the sun
until the sun sets

and then when it's night
the flowers unwind
calmly        slowly        never fast
sunflowers
turn back in the dark

at dawn the next day
what will the sun see
the sun will see me
asleep in a sunflower sea

**Soon**

are you coming          in a minute
means this minute        means a while

but if they say        I've got time
it's supper soon      to play and play

## Real

moms's asleep
she can't see me
and when I speak
she doesn't hear
I gently squeeze her ear
to tell her how I feel
**wake up, mom**
I want a mom who's real

## Three Days

daddy dropped me off
he gave me kisses for three nights
now he's at home and waiting there
for me
while I stay here
with cat and bear
I've got my bathrobe and my slippers
my flashlight's in my case
what we have for supper's up to me
but I can't make up my mind
maybe grandpa's special noodles
or else an ice-cream cake
but first of all I need to know
just how long do three days take

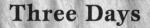

## Dancing

dust specks in a beam of light
a candle flickering at night
a goldfish in a goldfish bowl
a shadow dancing on the wall
a leaf that swirls down from a tree
and when I fall
asleep
the dancer in the dream
is me

## Silver and Gold

grandma is wrinkles
grandma is kind
grandma is cuddles
and grandma is old

her hair is made of silver
and her teeth are made of gold

## Like Grandpa

what are you looking at
what are you thinking of
what's got in your head

grandpa's hat is in my head
the one with the red feather
later on when grandpa's gone
there won't be anyone to wear it

and then I'll come and visit grandma
and put it on and look at her
and she'll say yes of course dear take it
and then I'll be a sir

# Night

it's dark and time for bed
I'm standing at the window
the cat next door has just gone out

the trees all sway
and tippety-tap
on the windowpane
as if to say
come out and play

it's not allowed
it's much too late
the clouds are turning black
the street is one big shadow

the cat next door meows
and wants to come back in
I close the curtains
let nighttime begin

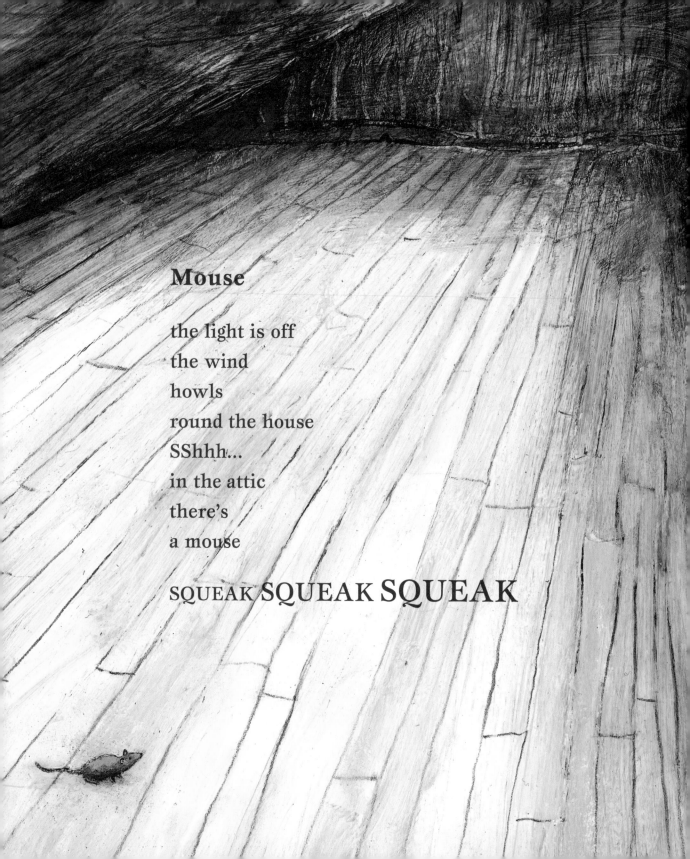

## Mouse

the light is off
the wind
howls
round the house
SShhh...
in the attic
there's
a mouse

SQUEAK SQUEAK SQUEAK

## Stars

far far far away
the sky is full
of little stars
too many stars
to ever count
for someone small like me

the longer I look
the more I see
as if the little baby stars
all come out just for me

## Arrows

white weather
woolen mittens
winter coat

where yesterday
the grass still showed
I see arrows
in the snow
and those arrows
lead the way
to a bird
that's all alone

my breath's a cloud
a white shout
rings out

fly   bird   fly

# Enough

a thousand trees in a forest
a thousand drops in the rain
and in the lawn
a thousand blades of grass
but
how many words have I got left
how many tears, how many laughs
how many bubbles of spit
how many goodnight kisses
will I still get
how many will I give

enough
to last a lifetime
to last as long as I live